Rainbow
ANIMAL HOSPITAL

Trash Cat's Secret

Rainbow ANIMAL HOSPITAL

Trash Cat's Secret

Steve Attridge

Collins
An imprint of HarperCollinsPublishers

Rainbow
ANIMAL HOSPITAL

by Steve Attridge

For my son, Jacob. Also, thanks to staff at the Avonvale Veterinary Group, Warwick, for their help. Any factual errors remain mine alone.

First published in Great Britain 1996 by Collins

3 5 7 9 8 6 4

Collins is an imprint of
HarperCollins*Publishers* Ltd
77-85 Fulham Palace Road, London W6 8JB

Copyright © Steve Attridge 1997

The moral right of the author has been asserted.

ISBN 0-00-675243-8

Printed and bound in Great Britain by
Caledonian International Book Manufacturing Ltd., Glasgow G 64

Chapter One

A FAMILIAR FACE

"I thought tortoises were meant to be dead slow," said Eddie. "This one's more like Linford Christie."

Hilary David laughed at the female tortoise called Charlie, who was about the size of a saucer, lumbering for all she was worth across the X-ray plate. It surprised Eddie how quick and nimble a tortoise could be. Eddie caught her deftly in both hands and returned her to the centre of the plate. The owner of the tortoise had brought her into the hospital that morning because she had a lump on her neck and for the past ten minutes Hilary had been trying, unsuccessfully, to take an X-ray. Charlie refused to keep still. In fact, she was extremely angry, spitting and straining and hissing every time she was picked up and returned to the centre of the plate. The X-ray machine was the size of a large overhead projector, and kept in the prep room where animals were usually prepared for operations that would be done in the theatre next to it. Eddie sometimes watched different animals having parts of their bodies shaved in readiness, and saw the autoclave, a large oven-like machine

in the corner, being loaded with instruments and bowls to be sterilised. He had not yet been allowed to watch an actual operation. But this tortoise who wouldn't keep still was another first.

"I could hold her," said Eddie.

"Then we might end up with an X-ray of your hand," said Hilary.

It was a problem. How could they keep Charlie still for a moment?

Eddie thought hard. Sometimes, if he had a real problem, he would say what it was to himself, not aloud but silently, then count to ten. If he was lucky, the solution appeared to plop into his brain like magic. He had picked up this trick from his little sister Kate, who, despite being only seven, seemed to have a vast knowledge of how the human brain worked. She was also a good fighter and a good laugh. The counting to ten didn't always work, but it was certainly worth a try. He tried it now. He said what the problem was, then counted, one, two, three, four, five, six, seven, eight, nine, ten.

"Sellotape!" he said.

"Excellent idea," said Hilary. Eddie held Charlie, while Hilary got some sticky tape from her office. She cut two long strips and crisscrossed them over Charlie's shell and onto the X-ray plate.

Charlie was furious. She spat and hissed and tried to use her powerful legs to free herself, but it was no use. Like it or not, there she was, stuck fast. Eddie moved behind the protective wall as Hilary lowered the hood of the X-ray machine. She stepped back to join Eddie, her thumb ready to press the switch at the end of the extension lead she was holding. The X-ray flashed on Charlie for a moment.

"There, you can put her in the ward now, Eddie, and when I develop the negative we'll see how big this lump is."

Eddie took Charlie back to the ward and put her in one of the cages fixed to the wall. In the cage below was a beautiful terrier dog, a golden colour with a thick fringe almost covering his eyes. It was his eyes that were the problem. Greg, the nursing assistant, was bathing them three or four times a day until surgery was performed. The dog, called Frisk, had a rare problem; his eyelashes curled over and grew into his eyes. If untreated, the dog could go blind, slowly and painfully.

Eddie tickled his nose through the wire of the cage, then went off to the smaller ward to see his rabbit, Thumper, for whom he had been given special responsibility until the rabbit was strong enough and an owner could be found for it. Of course, Eddie very much hoped that no owner would be found – ever. Although he didn't know it, all the staff at Rainbow Animal Hospital, except Mr Wensleydale, had agreed to keep Thumper as a permanent resident because Eddie had grown so attached to him. He was now several months old and, apart from being a little on the small side, seemed perfectly healthy. Eddie took him out of his hutch and gave him a kiss on the nose. Thumper licked Eddie's face enthusiastically. Eddie put him down and laughed as the rabbit lolloped round and round his feet.

Hannibal the bulldog trundled in on his squeaky chariot, a special form of transport that had been made for him after his back legs had been crushed in a road accident. Hannibal was another of Eddie's special friends at the hospital and the two of them watched approvingly as Thumper enjoyed his youth and newly acquired health. Not long ago Thumper had been a pathetic little character, full of shivers and fear. Now it looked as though he was going to be exactly the kind of independent and roguish personality that Eddie liked, a bit like Eddie himself, in fact.

The morning was passing quickly. It was half-term and Eddie had been at the hospital every day except Wednesday when he played in a football match. Eddie found that time moved at different speeds in different places. In school, for example, it often slowed down to a dawdle. When you are asleep it seemed to stop. If you are having a really cool time then, unfairly, time seemed to go much faster. Time at the hospital always went fast, because there was always something happening, always something to be done, always another animal to be looked after. Like now, with Thumper and Hannibal. And down the corridor in the other ward, Eddie knew Kalim the nurse was feeding the patients; Hilary David was in her office writing up notes; in Reception, Eddie's sister Chelsea was constantly answering the telephone, updating files on the computer, and admitting new patients; and in the operating room, grumpy Mr Wensleydale was putting the final stitches in an Alsatian's leg that had been badly gashed on a piece of glass. Eddie would have liked to go and watch that, but he knew it was best to keep out of Mr Wensleydale's way. Old Cheesy, as Eddie called him, didn't approve of

Eddie's presence at the hospital. It was only the goodwill of Hilary, the other vet, that enabled him to be there most days of the week to help with the animals. Eddie had no idea why Old Cheesy didn't like him. As far as Eddie was concerned, his own personality was brilliant! But, whatever the reason, Cheesy didn't share that opinion.

Only a few days ago Eddie had asked Chelsea why she thought Old Cheesy had such serious personality problems. She said he had a 'character bypass operation, like a lot of men', whatever that meant. She also said he was very worried because the hospital was having financial problems and if they got any worse they might have to get rid of some of the staff, perhaps even close the hospital. This was serious. This was impossible. Eddie promised himself it wouldn't happen, not if he could help it. He would give the matter some serious thought. He did think they could contact the local MP and ask him to help, but only the other day Eddie had heard Mr Wensleydale describe the local MP as a turnip-head.

Eddie went through to Reception. It was time for lunch. Maybe he could persuade Chelsea to take him to McDonald's. He'd have a hamburger with no onions or relish, a large fries, a regular coke—

Suddenly, Eddie's thoughts were interrupted. He stopped and stared.

It was the cat he recognised first. It was the big ginger tom called Trash Cat that belonged to Eddie's friend, Imran. Greg was heading towards one of the consulting rooms, holding Trash in his arms.

"I know that cat. What's up with her?" Eddie asked, hoping it was nothing serious.

"Can't stop," said Greg as he rushed on by. "But it's serious."

Eddie tried Chelsea.

"What's wrong with that cat?" Eddie asked.

"Which one?" asked Chelsea. She was trying to fill in admission forms for two other cats. She was hungry and whenever Chelsea was hungry she got in a bad mood. She was obviously going to have to wait for lunch. No McDonald's for me either, Eddie thought. He was just rushing out of the hospital to go round to Imran's when they almost ran smack into each other.

"How's Trash? Where is she? My mum brought her in. I've only just found out. She's not going to die, is she?" asked a breathless Imran.

"No, no of course she's not," said Eddie, who had no idea at all what was wrong with Trash, or whether or not she would die.

Chapter Two

WHAT'S WRONG WITH TRASH?

"There is definitely something there," said Hilary, as she gently touched different parts of Trash's abdomen. Trash was lying on her side, looking very sorry for herself, her gingery-green eyes almost closed. Imran stroked her head while she was being examined. Eddie looked at the perfect markings on her body; ginger, the colour of burnished gold, with perfect fawn zigzags like miniature cartoon bolts of lightning on her shoulders. Eddie wanted to feel Trash's abdomen, too, but decided he had better take a back seat while Hilary was working. She was his ally in getting round the bad-tempered Mr Wensleydale. It was best to keep in Hilary's good books, and try not to ask too many questions while the vet was concentrating on her diagnosis. Funnily enough, Eddie had discovered that sometimes, by not asking for something, he got it anyway. Like now.

"Here, Eddie. Feel here. Gently," said Hilary, guiding Eddie's fingertips to a spot in Trash's abdomen.

"Feel anything?" she asked.

"I'm not sure. Yes, yes, just there," said Eddie, who could feel a small lump.

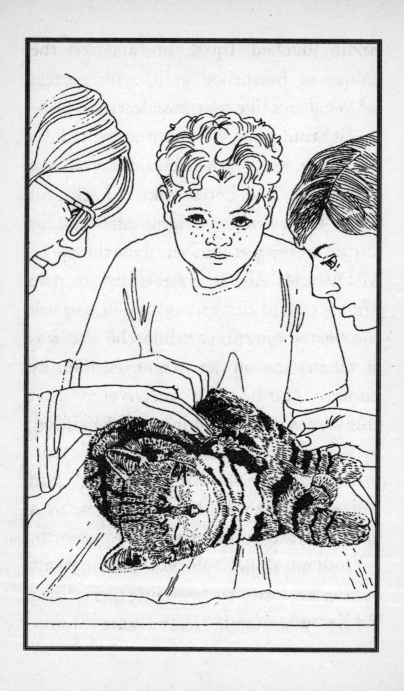

Imran touched Trash too, and felt the lump.

"What is it?" Eddie asked.

"Difficult to say," Hilary answered.

"Why can't you just X-ray her to see what's there?" asked Eddie.

He was aching to show Imran that he knew how to use the X-ray machine.

"Difficult to see anything in the tummy with an X-ray, it's all packed together so tightly in there. X-rays are much better with the chest, or legs, or head.

"Surgery?" asked Eddie. He could see that Imran was pretty impressed with this professional conversation he was having with a proper vet, and he was determined to milk it for all it was worth.

"I don't think so. Not yet anyway. Some people are far too eager to perform exploratory surgery. They forget it's very traumatic for the animal. I'd rather wait a bit and see what happens. We'll try her on a high dose of castor oil, as a purgative. If she's swallowed something, that should help her to pass it."

"If it does what I think it will, I'm keeping well out of the way," said Imran. "And it tastes disgusting."

"Not if you're a cat," said Hilary.

She asked Imran if he'd noticed Trash eating anything out of the ordinary, or being sick. He hadn't. She asked if the road where he lived had been repaired recently. He said it hadn't and wanted to know why she asked.

"Because some animals seem to like the taste of tar. We had a Labrador in here last year who had twenty-three stones from the road in his stomach. He'd licked the tar and swallowed the stones. He'd become a sort of addict."

Trash was given a mild painkiller, then a large spoonful of castor oil. Hilary took her to the large ward and put her in a cage, then left Eddie and Imran with her. Trash promptly rolled over and went to sleep. It seemed that the mystery of Trash's lumpy tummy was to remain a mystery, at least for the present.

Eddie took Imran off to see Hannibal for a slobbery cuddle, then they took Thumper out for a game. The little rabbit was turning out to be a skilful footballer, a talent which Eddie insisted Thumper had somehow magically inherited from him. Eddie took a ball from his pocket and placed it in front of Thumper.

"Come on, Tumps, do the business," encouraged Eddie.

Thumper nuzzled the ball with his quivering whiskers, then he gave it a little push with his nose, then another push.

Eddie placed his foot in front of the ball and Thumper neatly nosed the ball around his foot.

"Excellent," said Imran.

"Comes from being a Dutch rabbit," said Eddie. "Dutch players are always good on the ball. Exceptional dribbling skills."

"Brazilians are best," said Imran.

"Not the rabbits, though," said Eddie confidently. "If you want real ball skills, it's definitely your Dutch rabbit to go for. If I could find Thumper's brothers and sisters I could get up a team."

Imran stroked Thumper's silky ears, which immediately flattened against his head.

"You're dead lucky being able to come here so much," said Imran, who was rarely impressed by anything.

"Well, they recognise my superior

intelligence and skill. They rely on me all the time," said Eddie.

"Yeah, sure, now just wait there while I widen the door so we can get your head through it," said Imran.

"Don't move in case you step on her!" said Greg, as they came in. He was down on his hands and knees looking under a cupboard.

"What is it?" asked Eddie.

"Charlie's escaped," said Greg.

Chapter Three

THE DISAPPEARING PATIENT

Eddie and Imran jumped into action. As Greg explained, there were two crises. The most important was Charlie's disappearance, the second was not to let Mr Wensleydale know what had happened. If he discovered that one of the patients had escaped, someone's head would roll, probably several, including Greg's. It seemed to Eddie that this was one of the many things wrong with Old Cheesy's brain; its failure to know that sometimes things just happened. People did odd things, objects moved from where you put them, good ideas suddenly became bad ones. There were no logical reasons to explain these things. They just happened. Eddie looked at Charlie's open cage and decided that this could be one of those impossible-to-explain-so-don't-even-bother-trying things. Charlie had been there. Somehow she got out. Now she was gone. But where? That was the important question for the moment.

Greg and Imran looked in the ward, in all the cages, on top of them, in the corners, on the shelves. Nowhere. Eddie went out into the back yard and looked around the large dustbins, the walls and gate, around a mysterious looking and padlocked shed. Eddie, who seemed to move more quickly than most people, then ferreted around the smaller ward and in the storeroom. Then he stopped to think. Sometimes that was the best way to find something, or someone – not to charge around in a panic, but to stop and think carefully. Charlie had been in a foul mood, so she would want to get away quickly. That meant she probably wouldn't stay in the ward where she had been kept. She had been fed so she probably wouldn't be hungry and in search of food. Eddie knew tortoises were intelligent reptiles with an uncanny sense of direction. If she came across something that interested her, she might well investigate. Charlie was also stubborn. If she wanted to get somewhere, she would. What else?

Tortoises like shelter. Secret places. Warm places. Where might that be?

Eddie had another quick look in the storeroom, then wandered out and into the corridor. Where was somewhere warm? Somewhere where there was heating. There was heating all over the hospital. It was essential, especially for very poorly animals. Charlie could be anywhere. . . . Bedding – that was warm. But Eddie had already looked in the stores where blankets, newspaper and the special hospital bedding that looked like white bath mats were kept. Where else? Well, when the blankets and things needed washing they were piled up in the utility room and left until the next wash. That was it! Somewhere warm and safe. Eddie mentally bet his next three week's pocket money that Charlie would be in the utility room.

The washing machine was chugging away and there was a warm, soapy smell of washing powder and clean linen. In the corner was a huge pile of dirty things.

"Charlie?" called Eddie.

Carefully, he started to lift things off the remaining pile of smelly laundry. Maybe Charlie had managed to conceal herself right at the bottom. There were blankets, towels, tea towels, cloths, white sheets, a few dog coats, some washable elastic bandages, but no tortoise. Eddie got right down to the last blanket and lifted it. No Charlie.

That was it, then. Charlie had apparently disappeared into thin air.

Eddie was at a loss to know where else to look when he sensed a movement and saw something out of the corner of his eye. He turned and there, just leaving the utility room, was a walking tea towel, with a map of Wales on its hump. Eddie grinned and followed it into the corridor.

The tea towel marched along the corridor with Eddie behind. Ron, the ambulance driver came out of the rest room and started walking towards Eddie. Ron saw the tea towel and stopped. He looked at the towel, at Wales, then at Eddie.

"Just giving her some exercise," said Eddie as they passed.

Ron nodded feebly. He'd learnt that there were times when it was best to ignore what went on around Eddie, and he decided that this was one of those times. If Eddie Wright was exercising a tea towel then that was fine by him. He wasn't going to interfere. He walked on, fighting down his curiosity.

The tea towel continued its journey,

heading towards Reception with Eddie following. The tea towel bumped into a fire door. Eddie opened it and the tea towel plodded through and into Reception. Chelsea looked up from her computer and a man sitting with his dog noticed the tea towel. He nudged the person next to him and soon everyone was watching the map of Wales slowly make its way purposefully towards the front door. Eddie had the giggles but was managing to stifle them. The tea towel was starting to slip a little and Wales was beginning to slide onto the floor. Just as it reached the front door and was about to make its bid for freedom, Eddie reached down and lifted it. Charlie's head popped out just below Cardiff and she hissed fiercely at Eddie.

"Sorry, Charlie, but it's a fair cop," he said and turned to take her back to the

ward, leaving Chelsea bemusedly shaking her head.

Once Charlie was safely back in her cage, Eddie and Imran went to check on Trash. The cat was up and prowling about in her cage like a puma. This wasn't the Trash who had seemed to be at death's door a remarkably short time ago.

Greg smiled. "Pretty good, eh?" he said.

"Amazing," said Imran.

Imran lifted the big ginger cat out of the cage. Trash purred and nuzzled him, looked slyly at Eddie, then playfully tried to paw his face, her claws withdrawn to show it was a game. Hilary was called to see if she thought Trash really was all right. She examined Trash's abdomen.

"Feels fine," she said. "Has she done

her business?"

"Oh. Yes. But I cleaned out the cage and threw it all—" Greg's voice faded as he realised he'd made a mistake.

"What's up?" asked Imran.

"Trash had a blockage. The castor oil was to try and move it, whatever it was. And if it came out, I wanted to examine it," said Hilary.

"What – you mean rummage through her doings?!" asked Imran.

"That's exactly what I mean," said Hilary, smiling at Imran's horrified face.

"I'm sorry," said Greg.

"Don't worry, I should have told you. I just didn't expect it to happen so quickly," said Hilary.

Chapter Four

TRASH'S FAVOURITE GAME

Half an hour later, Eddie, Imran and Trash were at Imran's house, drying out. They had got halfway back when the skies had opened and it rained like a monsoon. They met Eddie's sister, Kate, who was out in the street with the rain falling on her upturned face.

"Why are you doing that?" Imran asked.

"Because it feels good," Kate replied, doing a little rain dance in a puddle.

"Where are you going?" she asked.

"Back to Imran's for lunch," Eddie said.

The mention of lunch took Kate's mind off the rain and she went with them. Imran wasn't too happy about this as he thought Kate was a bit loony. But he also knew if she wanted to do something, it was best not to try and stop her. He'd seen the results of other kids' disputes with her – bruised shins, ears ringing from shouting, the odd fat lip.

Before going back to work, Imran's mother opened a special get-well tin of sardines for Trash and made beans on toast for Imran, Eddie, Kate and Imran's little brother, Ranjit. He was six and

Imran called him Hamster because he had such chubby cheeks. This infuriated Ranjit. Eddie thought it was rather a compliment to be likened to a hamster; they were friendly, beautiful little animals. But he knew better than to interfere too much with the constant bickering and sometimes epic arguments between Imran and Ranjit. Brothers were meant to like each other but sometimes they just didn't. Imran and Ranjit not only didn't like each other, they lost no opportunity in letting everyone know they didn't. Today, it was obvious that a major battle was brewing. Eddie gulped down his lunch so he could get away before he was drawn into it too.

"You did take them!" shouted Imran.

"What would I want with your useless marbles?" sneered Ranjit, showing a mouthful of half-chewed beans.

"Marbles is a rubbish game."

"That's probably why you took them, then. Because you're rubbish! And you look like a hamster with your puffy fat cheeks," said Imran.

"And you've got a nose like a rat's bottom," shouted Ranjit.

Kate settled down with a smile. With any luck this argument might develop into a proper fight. Eddie decided it was time to beat a retreat. The row would go on for hours, and the quality of insults would get worse, if that was possible, which he doubted. He went upstairs to Imran's room, thinking he might have a go at one of his mega drive games, perhaps *Street Fighter Two*, or the UEFA cup game that Imran always infuriatingly won.

Eddie was sitting on the floor going through the games and turning over in his mind the problem of how to raise money for the hospital. Trash, who was spying on him from the top bunk, suddenly decided to attack. She took a flying leap and landed on Eddie's head, sending him sprawling across the floor on his back. After the initial shock, Eddie laughed as Trash now sat on his stomach elegantly washing her paws. Eddie imagined that she had a creamy voice with words that ended in purrs or hisses.

"Sssssoooooo, you want to purr-lay the funny gamesssss. Yesssss?" he said.

Eddie picked Trash up, noticing how supple her body was and how her spine could coil right round, almost like a snake. He put her on a shelf containing videos. She seemed to sense that something interesting was about to happen and sat quite still, her gingery-green eyes watching Eddie with great

concentration. Eddie took a mangy-looking sock from under the bunk bed and rolled it into a ball. He found a piece of string in one of Imran's pockets and tied it around the sock. Then he lay on the bed and looked up at Trash on the shelf about two metres away. For a moment they both listened to the rain beating on the window panes. Trash didn't once divert her gaze from him.

"OK. Let's see just how good you are, Trash," said Eddie. "One, two, three," and he flicked the sock out. Trash leapt from the shelf but just missed the sock as Eddie flicked the string back.

"Not bad, but you can do better," said Eddie.

He put Trash back on the shelf and tried again.

"One, two, three," and a flick of the string. The sock flew out and Trash made a spectacular leap, landing like a panther but missing the sock by a fraction as Eddie flicked it back. He tried again. This time, Trash was all fired up and ready. Even before Eddie had flicked the string, she jumped, only to find nothing there. Eddie had fooled her this time by only pretending to flick out the sock. He laughed as Trash's tail gave an angry little twitch. Eddie put her back on the shelf. She licked her paw, looked up at the ceiling and yawned as if the last thing she was interested in was this silly game. In fact, she was paying very close attention, trying to lull Eddie into a false sense of security. He counted "One, two, three," and flicked the sock out. Trash was on it in a trice. She clamped the sock down with her paws, then picked it up in her mouth triumphantly and tossed it aside.

Eddie was very impressed. He patted

and stroked her head and she nuzzled the palm of his hand.

It all seemed quiet downstairs now. Eddie decided to go and see if the battle of the brothers was over.

It was. Ranjit was sulking and scowling and Imran was eating a chocolate bar. Kate had got fed up with them and gone home.

"Fancy a game of football on the mega drive?" Eddie asked.

"Sure," said Imran. "It's a while since I've beaten you. Promise not to cry. Is Trash up there?"

"Yes," said Eddie. "She's fine now. Fit as anything."

As usual, the two friends raced each other up the stairs two or three at a time. They burst through Imran's door and came to a standstill. Trash was rolling about on the carpet. At first, Eddie thought she was playing, but she wasn't. She was in agony.

Chapter Five

HERE WE GO AGAIN

Eddie kept cool and Imran didn't. Eddie telephoned the hospital, but Chelsea told him Ron was already out on an emergency call and it would be quicker to get Trash to the hospital themselves. Imran was on the floor telling Trash not to die. Ranjit had come upstairs and was kneeling beside them, crying.

Imran took a small rug from the bottom bunk, gently put it round Trash and lifted her into the pet carrier that Eddie had brought up from the kitchen. She was very still and her top lip was pulled back in a strange grimace that was almost a grotesque smile. Eddie had seen that sort of look only once before – on a cat that had been run over. The memory of the cat's face flashed before him, but he pushed it down so that he could think clearly.

"Ring for a cab. Quick!" he told Imran.

Imran seemed to snap out of a trance. He raced downstairs and flicked through the Yellow Pages until he found TAXIS. He telephoned the first number while Eddie brought the pet carrier downstairs.

Ranjit had stopped crying and was now full of annoying questions. "Why is Trash pulling that face? Will she be all right? Where do animals go when they die? Can I come to the hospital?" Luckily, a neighbour called round just as they were leaving, so Ranjit went next door. Eddie was glad. He had enough to worry about without another raging row between Imran and Ranjit in the cab.

The cab driver looked at the pet carrier.

"Sorry, son. No pets in the cab."

Eddie ignored him and got into the cab. Imran followed.

"Rainbow Animal Hospital. And step on it. This is an emergency!"

Eddie had always wanted to say that... and now he had.

"Why didn't you say so in the first place? Used to have a rat meself. Ferris his name was. Broke me heart when he had a heart attack from overeating. Mind you, my old mum's steak and kidney pud was

enough to kill off a small bull elephant, let alone a rat. Still heartbreaking, though. I remember his little whiskery nose all twitching just before he'd bite a lump out of me finger. Very sweet it was . . ."

As the cab splashed through the rain, the driver kept up this monologue about the death of Ferris all the way to the hospital, which is just what Eddie and Imran, and presumably Trash, did not want to hear.

At the hospital Eddie and Imran took Trash straight through to Hilary's treatment room. They had got soaked just running from the cab to the hospital door and left a trail of wet footprints. Hilary joined them a few moments later. She had been helping Greg and Kalim to move food and medicines out of the storeroom because rain had started to seep in through the roof and down the wall. Hilary and Mr Wensleydale had argued only recently about how to spend the hospital budget. Hilary wanted to use most of it on new equipment, while Mr Wensleydale was all for making repairs to the hospital on the grounds that there was no point in having new equipment if you didn't have a hospital to put it in.

Hilary lifted Trash from the pet carrier very gently. Trash was subdued and immediately lay down. Hilary realised this was probably because being in pain is very tiring, and eventually animals, like people, can become exhausted by it and appear to give up. It all becomes too much. This is a critical time, because giving up can literally mean that. Hilary felt Trash's stomach but couldn't find anything obvious.

"Anything?" asked Imran.

"Not yet," said Hilary.

She didn't know if this was something new or a recurrence of the old problem. It could be a tumour, of course, rather than something Trash had eaten, in which case surgery would be essential. Food poisoning would not have worn off, then come back in this way. She thought to herself how so much of medicine was a mixture of knowledge and intelligent guesswork.

"If only we knew what it was," she said, more to herself than to either of the boys.

Eddie had his eyes closed and was counting to ten.

Suddenly, he knew. Suddenly it was obvious. Why hadn't he thought of it before?

"I know what it is. I know what's wrong with Trash," he said.

Hilary and Imran both stared at him.

Chapter Six

JUST IN TIME

"Marbles!" said Eddie.

"I beg your pardon?" said a bemused Hilary.

"Trash has swallowed some marbles. I don't know how many, but that's what happened. And that's what happened last time. Remember the argument you had with your brother, Imran?"

"Course," said Imran. "But it's him. He keeps nicking them."

"And you searched his room?" asked Eddie.

"His room, his clothes, all his toys. Everywhere," said Imran.

"And you didn't find them," said Eddie. "Did you?"

"Well . . . No," admitted Imran. "But maybe he threw them away. Maybe he took them to school."

"Don't you think it's a bit of a coincidence that both times you've lost the marbles recently were just before Trash got ill?"

Imran hated conceding defeat, even when he was beaten. He just shrugged his shoulders.

"Maybe," he said, grudgingly.

"It's possible. I've known cats that

have eaten strange things in my time – buttons, bits of crayon, even a safety pin once," said Hilary. "But what is clear is that Trash is in a lot of pain. If whatever is causing it, marbles or not, doesn't move fairly soon, I shall have to operate."

Hilary gave Trash another huge dose of castor oil and left Imran and Eddie to watch her for half an hour. Hannibal came to snuffle and slobber, offering his own brand of comfort and support. Eddie stroked his ears, and the folds of flesh around his chops. Hannibal was always very much there, very solid and real.

Trash lay on her side with her eyes closed. Imran stroked her head, making little twisting patterns in the ginger fur with his fingertips. Her breathing was very short, her chest barely moving at all.

It reminded Eddie of when he was ill with bronchitis. It hurt to breathe too deeply, so you took little shallow breaths. Perhaps Trash was doing that. He listened to the rain drumming outside and tried to hear words in the sound of it: *DUM-DUM-DUM-DUM-DUM-DUM-DUM – GET-BET-TER-TRASH-GET-BET-TER-TRASH*

Trash's eyes were flickering and Eddie saw the strangeness of the double set of eyelids that cats have. He wondered if Trash was dreaming, perhaps about her favourite jumping game, or about stretching then curling up in front of a radiator. Her nose was curled into her bottom in that clever way animals have of making a circuit with their bodies to contain warmth. There was so much to learn just by looking at animals. It would take several lifetimes just to begin to understand a few animals, let alone all of them.

A few rooms away in his office, Mr Wensleydale was going through the accounts. It always amazed him how much everything cost once you added it all up – food, dressings, equipment, the mortgage on the hospital, bedding, computer maintenance, heating and lighting, staff salaries. There was more money going out every month than there was coming in. Eventually something would have to give. He may even have to consider losing one of the staff. Could they do without a receptionist? Not really. Without Chelsea the whole administration would collapse. They needed Ron for the ambulance. Two vets were the absolute minimum. Hilary would have to stay, even though there were moments when that little look of superioriority crossed her face and he would have been quite happy to see her go. Perhaps it would have to be one of the nursing staff, Greg or Kalim. Greg hadn't taken his finals yet, so was less qualified, but that also meant his salary was less. Mr Wensleydale was aware that he himself was not exactly the most popular man in the world. But he wasn't here to be popular, he told himself, he was here to do a job. Nevertheless, he felt more gloomy than usual. And that rain! Thundering down outside. The storeroom was leaking, the roof needed repairs. More expense, more worry.

In the ward, Eddie was also turning over in his mind the problem of money. An idea was beginning to form. No more than an idea at present but one worth leaving in his mind to see if it would grow or still seem as good in a few hours time. He would try it out on Kate. She was always good at judging if an idea was good, or simply a bundle of nothings. He went off to have a five minute play with Thumper and check on the patients in the other ward. Kalim was feeding them. Charlie the tortoise was trying to claw her way out of her cage, pausing only to cast her beady eyes over Eddie, as he tried to tickle her nose. The terrier dog with ingrowing eyelashes had had his operation and his eyelids were covered with cream to help them heal. He had a white contraption strapped to his head, like a bucket with the bottom missing, to stop him scratching his eyes with his paws. He still wasn't used to it and every time he turned around he banged his head on the side of his cage.

"Hello, bucket-head," said Eddie.

"Watch this," said Kalim.

She put some biscuits in the terrier's cage and as he bent to eat them the bucket rested on the floor, clamped over the food bowl, so that his head was completely hidden under the bucket. It was the perfect device for making sure no one else could get your dinner. Kalim and Eddie laughed. She was usually a bit cool with Eddie, probably taking her cue from Mr Wensleydale. Perhaps, at last, she was beginning to see that he was all right. Who knows? Eddie thought. Adults were a mystery and often best left that way. Even if you spent ages trying to work out what they were doing and why, it often wasn't worth the effort anyway. Life was too short to spend a lot of time understanding people, and not long enough to understand everything about animals.

*

Finally the half hour was up and Eddie went back to see Trash. Imran was still gently stroking her head. Eddie didn't think he'd ever seen Imran stay in one place for so long. Hilary came quickly into the room and began to examine Trash's abdomen. The lump hadn't moved. If anything, it seemed more solid. She was sure she could feel several lumps, small, hard and round, just like marbles, and they didn't seem at all interested in moving. Trash's mouth and throat were becoming dry. It was time to act.

"I'm going to operate," said Hilary quietly.

Eddie saw Imran's eyes well with tears, but he let his friend turn away to recover himself. If a friend didn't want to be seen crying, then you should leave him alone, he thought. And so the preparations for the operation began.

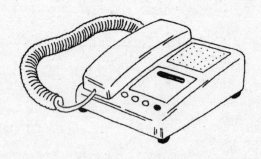

Chapter Seven

OPERATION AND A DISASTER

Imran carried Trash into the prep room where she was laid carefully on a trolley. Then Kalim, who was to assist in the operation, came to weigh Trash. She had to gauge exactly the right amount of anaesthetic to give her – too much and she would be too drugged and that might affect her recovery; too little and she would remain conscious and might become distressed during the operation. Then Hilary told Imran how all the instruments and equipment she would use had been sterilised in the autoclave to reduce the risk of infection.

While Kalim shaved an area about the size of a large egg on Trash's side, so that her fur wouldn't get in the way, Hilary showed Imran the operating theatre. It was about the size of a smallish bedroom, with an operating table in the middle under a big adjustable light. There was only one door and Hilary explained that this too reduced the risk of infection by limiting the amount of coming and going. People couldn't use the room as a thoroughfare when it wasn't being used for surgery.

"She'll be all right, Imran. Don't

worry," Hilary said to reassure him.

Then Imran and Eddie went back to the ward to wait. Eddie desperately wanted to watch an operation, but so far, no one had offered him the opportunity. Now, when his friend's cat was seriously ill, didn't seem like a good time to ask.

"She's a cool vet," said Eddie. "They don't come any better. Take it from me. Trash will probably like it so much she'll want to come back for another operation. Look on the bright side – at least this way you'll get your marbles back!"

Imran smiled, and they went to Reception to see if Chelsea would let them raid the staff biscuit tin. Eddie also wanted to use the telephone.

"Who do you want to phone?" asked Chelsea.

Eddie tapped the side of his nose

knowingly.

"People. Just people."

"About what?"

"Things. Just things," said Eddie, gaining some pleasure from the fact that this was winding Chelsea up. Winding people up was one of Eddie's favourite pastimes.

In the operating theatre, Trash was entering a very peaceful sleep, lying on her back, her head to one side. Kalim held her head and regulated the mask. Hilary worked quietly and efficiently. Neither of them spoke. The relentless sound of rain pounding on the roof seemed to be getting louder and louder. Will it never stop? Hilary was thinking.

Eddie made his telephone call. In fact he made three. One to his sister, Kate, who told him to go ahead with his idea, then two other calls. Chelsea tried to hear who Eddie was talking to, but he had deliberately turned his back to her and cupped his hand over the mouthpiece.

He is infuriating, thought Chelsea. Always some devious little scheme in mind, and always that *What Me?!* expression of innocent outrage when the latest scheme turns out to be a disaster. Chelsea could understand exactly why Eddie infuriated Mr Wensleydale. But he was her brother and she knew he could also be a lot of fun, even though he was just a kid. And there was no doubting that he was passionately devoted to the Animal Hospital.

Imran was on his fifth chocolate biscuit when Chelsea took the tin away. He began to look over the materials for sale in the exhibition area of Reception.

There were a lot of things for dogs and cats. Combs and brushes; a special long-handled toothbrush and toothpaste; flea collars and an advertisement for a new flea treatment in which the dog or cat takes a pill once a month; feeding bowls and dishes of all shapes and sizes; treats and nibbles that looked quite tasty. So tasty looking that Imran wouldn't have minded trying a few himself. Chelsea was dealing with a new patient and entering details into the computer. It was a bedraggled little poodle called Casper, with an ear infection. The dog's owner looked a bit like a poodle herself, with fluffy black hair and a small, anxious face.

Eddie joined Imran and Chelsea. "Bet you want to know what all that was about, don't you?" he asked with a big, smug grin on his face.

"Not at all," said Chelsea, who did want to know, really.

"Go on, ask me again," said Eddie.

"All right, what were your phone calls about?" Chelsea asked.

"Afraid I can't tell you," said Eddie, and he nodded at Imran to follow him. There might be some news about Trash.

They were halfway down the corridor when they heard an explosion from the big ward, followed by a shout, then a terrible rushing, swirling sound that Eddie couldn't identify. It sounded like the end of the world.

Chapter Eight

ALL HANDS ON DECK

As Eddie and Imran raced along the corridor a huge wave of water came whooshing along the corridor towards them. The filthy torrent gushed round their legs and flooded out into Reception. Just managing to keep their balance, they splashed through it to the storeroom which was now like a small but dirty swimming pool. Water nearly half a metre deep was swirling around inside and more was cascading down through a large ragged hole in the ceiling. Sodden cardboard boxes, bits of paper, and dozens of soggy tea bags were all bobbing about in the water.

"Quick! To the wards! The animals!" Eddie shouted above the roar of the water. He and Imran waded through to the smaller ward where there was less water but it still reached above their knees. There was another hole in the ceiling here. Water was pouring down in a dirty, browny-green waterfall, bringing with it all the filth and debris from the loft.

Against one wall, Mr Wensleydale was holding a cat in one arm and a dog in the other. His face was porcelain white and his thin hair, usually slicked back, was stuck to his forehead. He looks like a water vole, thought Eddie, suddenly feeling sorry for the man who was usually his worst enemy. But at this moment there were more important things than having enemies.

Other than damp and shock, there seemed to be no immediate danger to the animals in this ward. Then Greg shouted from the other, larger, ward.

"Help in here! Quickly!"

Everything seemed to speed up.

Eddie wades through the water and is just about to force his way through to the large ward when something crashes into him. Hannibal, floating like a hairy Roman god in his home-made chariot, his front legs paddling like fury. He yelps.

"All right, boy, it's all right boy. Good boy," soothes Eddie as he guides Hannibal back towards the corridor, where there is less water and Hannibal can paddle his way through to Reception. Now back through the smaller ward and to the large ward again. This is bad. Greg is trying to get all the lower cages out of the water. Here is the terrier with the bucket on his head, paddling water inside his cage. He is terrified. His eyes are a gluey, gooey, white mess as the ointment mixes with the water. Eddie opens the cage and hauls out the dog. What to do with him?

"Help me lift him!" Eddie shouts to Imran. Above is the cage with the cat who was in an accident. His tail has now been docked and is bandaged. The two boys lift the terrier and put him in with the startled cat. The animals stare at each other like two little lost refugees. Greg is taking the animals from the lower cages and putting them anywhere he can above the water. There is another cat on a shelf, dogs sharing cages. Greg struggles with the large Alsatian whose leg was gashed. Imran helps him to drag the dog outside

and into the corridor. They struggle to keep him afloat as he seems to have forgotten how to swim. A rabbit peeping over the edge of a cardboard box is teetering on the edge of being tipped into the water. Eddie pushes the box further back on the shelf. A rabbit? Thumper! Where is he? His cage is under water. Eddie reaches under the water and hauls

up the cage. The door is open. No Thumper.

"Thumper! Where are you?" Eddie cries. He gulps down air. His breath is coming in little gasps and he starts to feel hysterical. Where is Thumper? Eddie knows he has to keep calm if he is going to find his rabbit, but the panic is like a little gremlin inside him, jumping and screaming and sending him mad. He falls to his hands and knees and starts clawing about under the water. It is cold, freezing, and too dirty to see through. He feels over the slimy floor, dreading what he might find.

Chapter Nine

MORE WATERY PROBLEMS

In Reception, Chelsea had reacted quickly. She telephoned the fire brigade as soon as she realised what was happening. She ushered all the owners, who had been waiting with their sick pets, out of Reception. Some were still standing outside in the rain, gathering to

watch as people always do when there has been a disaster.

Now, Chelsea was urgently telephoning the owners of the in-patients to ask them to come and collect their pets. She was doing her best to reassure them, even though she herself was wondering why the fire brigade seemed to be taking so long. She also managed to keep stroking Hannibal's sodden head. At first Hannibal had been whimpering and wanting to get back to find Eddie, but he now seemed to have decided he could do most good by keeping out of the way, especially as Chelsea had found the biscuit tin and was absently feeding him one biscuit after another. In every disaster there is a little bit of good luck, Hannibal's wet, leathery, old face seemed to be saying.

*

Where was the fire brigade?

In the operating theatre Hilary was working as quickly as she could. The automatic safety switch had come on and shut down the electricity, or perhaps the water had got into a power point and fused the whole system. That meant no light, and there was only a small ceiling window in the theatre. Hilary was having to squint in the gloom. The shutdown also meant all the machinery was down and without more anaesthetic, Trash would soon be coming round. Kalim had gone to turn on the emergency generator which meant Hilary was having to work on her own. She took out another marble and added it to the five already in the little silver dish. No wonder Trash had been in pain. That was the last one.

Now Hilary set about putting in a few

neat stitches, her fingers working nimbly, almost as if they had little lives of their own. Luckily, the water wasn't too bad in here. Kalim had told her that there was literally a flood in the wards.

Hilary could guess what had happened. Rain leaking through the roof and into the loft, where it had been gathering all day until the pressure of its weight had found the weakest spot in the ceiling and crashed through. Once the ceiling was damp, then other weak spots would have given way. And now, all this damage. She dreaded to think about all the animals. Had they all survived? It was like being on Noah's Ark. And it was cold. Trash needed to be kept dry, warm and clean, like most of the animals, so what would they do? One problem at a time, she thought, putting in another tiny stitch. One problem at a time.

There was a tap at the door.

"Yes? Who is it?" asked Hilary.

"It's me, Imran. Is Trash all right?" he asked, afraid to come inside.

"Yes, she's going to be fine," said Hilary.

Mr Wensleydale had managed to get the animals from the smaller ward to positions of relative safety. Many of them were now in his office where there was only a few inches of water. They were in pet carriers and cages, perched on his desk and on shelves, anywhere where there was a dry space. Although he was sweating and breathing heavily he was aware that it was cold and the temperature was dropping. The flood water was very cold and all the heating had gone off when the electricity failed. He went back to the wards to see how

Greg and the boys were doing. Greg had gone to Reception to see how Chelsea was coping.

The fire brigade arrived moments later. One of the firemen splashed through the water and assessed the situation.

"I've seen worse. But not much worse. Keep all the doors open to let the water drain, and we'll start pumping. Do you need an ambulance?"

"No. I don't think anyone's hurt," said Mr Wensleydale. "We're just very wet, like the animals."

Within minutes two thick rubber pipes, connected to a suction pump outside on the fire engine, were ready to be switched on. One was in the smaller ward and one in the larger.

"Best stand to one side, son," said a fireman to Eddie, who was still frantically searching about in the watery mess.

"But if you start pumping he might get sucked up too!" said Eddie, his face streaming with dirt, water and tears.

"Who might?" asked the fireman.

"Thumper. My rabbit," said Eddie. "I can't find him."

"Look, son, you really shouldn't be here at all. This is dangerous, and if there was a rabbit here when the water came in, I'm afraid you've probably lost him," said the fireman.

"Oh, no! I completely forgot to tell you," said Greg, who had just returned from Reception.

Eddie stiffened. He had stopped breathing, desperately not wanting to hear what Greg was about to say.

"Sorry, Eddie," said Greg, reaching into his pocket and taking out a bewildered looking Thumper. "I put him in my pocket when the flood first started."

After being snuggled down for so long in the dark of Greg's pocket, the little rabbit blinked in the light.

"Tumps!" gasped Eddie, suddenly springing back to life and taking Thumper. He held him against his face, feeling the soft fur and tickle of whiskers.

"I thought I'd lost you, for ever," he whispered into Thumper's face. He could cope with anything now. Now he had Thumper back.

Within fifteen minutes the water had gone down to a few inches. The great pipes were sucking up the water like giant throats and spilling it into the drains outside. What was left was a dank, evil-smelling mush of sodden dust,

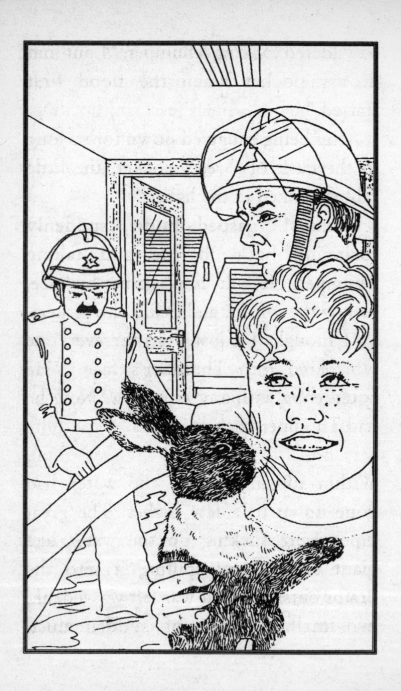

cobwebs, long-forgotten papers, and bat droppings from the loft, all littered with sodden bits of animal feed and bedding. It reminded Eddie of the canal whenever there was a hot summer and the canal was almost baked dry. What was left had one of the worst smells you could imagine. This was like that, but the slimy mess was still moving, swirling, as if it had a life of its own. Perhaps it did. Perhaps it *could* come alive. Perhaps this was some horrible *thing* trying to destroy the hospital, to get the animals, to get Thumper and Eddie! Anything was possible if you let yourself think about it.

Everything was wet, it was very cold and outside the rain was still pelting down.

Ron had arrived, bringing another problem with him – a box of abandoned kittens who looked very frightened and were probably very hungry.

"I'll get Chelsea to organise emergency repairs to the roof and ceiling," said Mr Wensleydale to Greg. "You see if you can get at least one of the wards habitable and we'll keep most of the animals in there for now. We may have to ferry them elsewhere."

"All the food and bedding is sodden. These animals are going to start dying on us unless we act quickly. Some, like the terrier, already look as if hypothermia is starting to set in," said Greg.

"I know that," Mr Wensleydale snapped. "But we can only deal with one crisis at a time. Any animals who are in real danger bring to me."

"I've got an idea," said Eddie.

Chapter Ten

EMERGENCY CHILD SUPPORT

A few minutes later, at Eddie's house, Kate was on the phone, listening intently to her brother. Her freckled face, framed by a halo of curls, was motionless in unblinking concentration.

"Yes, got it. All right, Eddie, just shut up now and do what you can. I'll start

Operation Hospital Support and be with you in about twenty-six and three-quarter minutes," said Kate. It was now 6p.m. and Kate was nothing if not precise.

"Yes, I know it's raining and some of them might not want to go out, but get serious, Eds. Are they going to argue with me or are they not? . . . Pre-cis-erly. I say it, they do it. It's the way of things. If not I'll bash them. That usually helps to persuade most kids."

Three minutes later, wearing her army combat parka and purple, size one Doc Martens, and with the rain still beating down, Kate was pounding on Jeremy Lambert's front door. Jeremy's mother opened it.

"Hello dear," she said. "I'm afraid Jeremy's a bit snuffly and can't come out."

"Mrs Lambert, if Jeremy isn't down here and ready to go in one minute, his life at school will be ab-so-luterly not worth living. He won't just be snuffly, he'll be snuffed."

Mrs Lambert looked shocked. She wasn't used to being talked to like this by seven-year-old girls. She was about to protest, but Kate raised her hand and stopped her.

"Just do it, Mrs Lambert. Lives are at stake."

"Whose lives?" asked Mrs Lambert, shocked. "Children's?"

"No. More important than that. Animals. And it involves my brother. Just get your son – I can't stand here yakking all night. And give him a few blankets and some old newspapers. Please!"

Thirty seconds later, Jeremy, with a

red, blocked nose and watery eyes, a big Manchester City scarf around his neck, was trudging along beside Kate. It was seven minutes past six.

"Jeremy, go and knock at Hattie Clodd's house. Get her to bring blankets, paper, and animal food. She's got two cats and a dog, so don't take no for an answer."

Jeremy went off while Kate went to another house and rang the bell. Sophie Smith answered the door. Kate's private view of Sophie was that she was a wimp, but in an emergency you take what you can get.

"Sophie, if you ask me any dumb questions I might lose my temper and you really wouldn't like that, I promise you. So just get your coat, all the dog food you can carry, and the blankets from your bed. Do it."

Sophie knew you didn't mess with Kate, so she did it. Kate sent Sophie off to get David Shore, while she called at Brenda Chan's. It was twelve minutes past six. At fifteen minutes past six she was having a mild disagreement with the bumptious Harry Seed Senior, father of Harry Seed Junior. Seed Senior was telling Kate that no way was his son going off to some grotty Animal Hospital to work for free. And anyway, it wasn't safe for children to be out on a night like this. There were some funny people about.

Kate was losing her patience.

"Mr Seed, let's look at your boy Harry, shall we? He picks his nose, he picks bits out of his ears, the last time he brushed his teeth, to judge by his pongy breath, was about three years ago. He slobbers his food all down his jumper, and his brain is mostly on holiday. Now, answer me one question. Would I be asking him if I wasn't absolutely desperate?"

Mr Seed was impressed.

"No, you wouldn't," he said.

And so Harry Seed Junior was summoned from an epic and, to his mind, succulent nosepicking session in the lavatory. A minute later he was walking along with Kate and the others. There were now twelve children, all carrying newspapers in bin liners, blankets, and boxes of animal food. Harry Seed had brought three giant packets of Weetabix. "For the budgies," he said. Kate was too busy to reply. The strange, slow workings of Harry's brain were best left untouched.

It was twenty minutes past six, and for once, the bus was on time. The children all piled on to it. Luckily Kate had thought to bring all the money from her piggy bank so she could pay for everyone.

At twenty-six and three-quarter minutes past six Kate and her band entered the Rainbow Animal Hospital, as Eddie knew they would. If Kate said something would happen, it would have to be something pretty important, like the end of the world, to stop it. They entered just after the first casualty of the day occurred.

Chapter Eleven

CLEARING UP

One of the kittens that Ron had brought in had died. Not from the flood, or the cold, but from the neglect it had already suffered before coming to the hospital. Chelsea wrapped the others in her coat and put them in the treatment room. The dead kitten she put in a box until it could be properly dealt with.

The builders had arrived and were stretching plastic sheeting over the roof as a temporary measure to keep out the rain. Inside the hospital it was still wet, slippery, foul-smelling and cold. Then Kate and the other children arrived. Mr Wensleydale was aghast.

"What on earth do you think you're doing?" he yelled at them. "We've got a major emergency on our hands here, and now we have a primary school outing arriving."

Hilary came to Reception to see what the fuss was about.

"I'm sorry," Chelsea was saying. "Kate's my sister. She's just trying to help."

"Are *all* the members of your family a nuisance?" stormed Mr Wensleydale.

A few of the children giggled as Kate

whispered, "Grumpbags. Must have thorns in his underpants."

"It's freezing in here," said Kate, quickly getting back to the task at hand.

"Yes. The generator packed up for a while. The emergency one is on, but the water has made everything damp and cold. And all the animal bedding is useless," said Kalim.

Kate looked at Sophie, Jeremy and David.

"You three take all the blankets and stuff and do what this lady says," she instructed them.

The three children followed Kalim down the corridor.

"Wait a minute! What do you think you're doing?" yelled Mr Wensleydale, who was beginning to feel his authority slipping away.

"Looks like they're trying to help,"

said Hilary.

"Ms David, if we'd had the repairs done when I suggested, none of this would have happened," Mr Wensleydale blustered.

"But you only made the suggestion last week, Mr Wensleydale. Hardly time for the repairs to have been done. In any case, perhaps we could have this discussion later," said Hilary. "For now, I think we need all the help we can get if we're going to save the animals."

"And what happens when one of these children gets hurt? More of the ceiling could fall down at any time. How would we explain that to their parents?" Mr Wensleydale asked, his face reddening as he heroically attempted to control his temper.

"If they want to help they could wear these," interrupted one of the builders.

He was holding a yellow safety helmet. "We've got loads of spares in the lorry, and like the lady says, looks like you need all the help you can get."

Even Mr Wensleydale could see the logic of this, and grudgingly assented but only if Hilary would get Chelsea to telephone the children's parents to explain what was happening and ask if it was OK for their children to stay and help. They would be trying to contact the owners of the animals, some of which would be collected, but the emergency was here and now, and they did need help. Some of the animals were not in a fit state to be moved and already Chelsea had worked out that many of the animals would not be collected because the owners were away or simply could not be contacted.

*

More work parties were formed. Imran was given the special duty of looking after Trash, given that she had only just had her operation. He sat with her in the treatment room, gently stroking her head as she started to come round.

Using the blankets and newspaper that the children had brought, Sophie, Jeremy and David were helping Kalim to make beds for the animals in Mr Wensleydale's and Hilary's offices. Now that the fire brigade had done the major work and left, four more children were given the task of mopping up the remaining water and muck that had come through the roof. The rest of the children were to be in charge of organising food for the animals. Harry Seed approached Kate.

"What can I do?" he asked.

"Just stop picking your nose and try to help mop up all this disgusting slobber

from the floor," Kate instructed him.

Harry looked quite pleased at the idea of getting down there in all the slobbery mess. Harry was definitely weird.

Kate and Eddie were to act as supervisors.

"I knew you'd get here," said Eddie.

"So did I," said Kate. "You look like the swamp monster."

Eddie looked down at himself. He was soaked, his clothes streaked with filth. His face looked as though it had been camouflaged. He smiled.

"It's going to be a long night," he said. "But at least, apart from that poor kitten, all the animals are safe at the moment." Then his face clouded.

"What is it?" Kate asked.

"Oh no! Charlie!" said Eddie. "I haven't seen her all day." He thrust Thumper into Kate's arms and ran off.

Chapter Twelve

Another Hunt for Charlie

Eddie went back to the wards. He had terrible pictures in his mind of Charlie being sucked up by the firemen's suction pipes, or of her being drowned and swept away. He looked in the yard outside, under the shed, behind the dustbins and under piles of bricks, where he had not yet been. Charlie wasn't in the yard. Charlie wasn't anywhere, it seemed. Then a thought struck Eddie.

He took a running slide along the corridor and skidded round to a sudden halt outside the utility room. There was still a few inches of murky water inside. He sploshed through to one of the big laundry baskets and lifted the lid. It was full of slightly damp towels and blankets. The lid had protected it from becoming really sodden, but there didn't seem to be any sign of Charlie.

Eddie lifted up a tea towel, then a blanket. Nothing. But there was a definite bump under the next towel. He lifted it and there was Charlie. At first Eddie thought she was dead, but then he realised she was in a deep, blissful sleep.

"Good for you, Charlie. You slept through it all."

He patted her shell gently, then picked her up to take her to Greg. How on Earth had she got into the basket? Another of those inexplicable mysteries, he thought with a grin.

A few hours later the hospital was starting to look a bit clearer. The builders were still clomping over the roof and had managed to stop most of the rain from coming in. A few owners had come to collect their pets, but there were still a lot of animals to look after. Some parents had come and taken home their children and, in some cases, one or two of the animal patients for the night. Kate, Eddie and Imran were determined to stay with Chelsea at the hospital all night. There were hot water bottles to keep filled, and the tropical fish tank in Reception would need monitoring to maintain the right temperature. Chelsea went home and did all the necessary persuading of their own parents and returned with sleeping bags and dry clothes. Mr Wensleydale did not like the idea of the children spending the night at the hospital, but in the end he was too exhausted to argue.

Both Mr Wensleydale's and Hilary's rooms were like wartime underground shelters. Everyone was huddled under blankets keeping warm and having whispered conversations. The only difference here was that most of those in the room were animals. Greg and Kalim had made hot chocolate and been out for hamburgers and fries. Eddie was now sitting up, wrapped in a blanket, with a steaming mug of chocolate and a large fries with ketchup, and Thumper was snuggled in with him. To his left was

Kate telling the bucket-headed terrier next to her a made-up story about a dog who became Prime Minister. To his right was Imran who was holding Trash wrapped in a white tea towel like a baby. Trash had come round from her operation but was still drowsy. Her eyes occasionally rolled as if she was in some strange dream world.

Eddie finished his drink and fries and thought about the day. It had seemed a hundred years long. He closed his eyes.

"Eddie! You awake?" hissed Imran.

But Eddie was in a watery dream, floating in a rickety old boat down a river that was becoming ever wider and faster. In the boat with him were animals of all shapes and sizes. Dogs, cats, hamsters, gerbils, rats, mice, cows, sheep, snakes. All sorts. Trash was sitting on a stretcher with a large bandage round her tummy, and eating fries from a paper cone. And there, at the helm and with his long ears poking through specially cut holes in a Captain's hat, was Thumper, his paws on the old-fashioned steering wheel. This was a much larger Thumper, man-sized, and with a serious but friendly expression on his face. Thumper turned to Eddie and said, "It's all right now. I've got the wheel. You go to sleep."

Imran looked down at Trash and realised how much he would have missed her if she had died. He also thought about Ranjit, his little brother, and what a pain he was. Nevertheless, he *hadn't* taken Imran's marbles and he would have to apologise. Imran would go home tomorrow and say he was sorry and Ranjit would probably smirk and say, "I told you so," and Imran would get mad and call him hamster chops and another big argument would break out. Their parents would tell them to stop it and Imran would storm up to his room in a huff and tell Trash Cat how unfair everything was. Yes, that's what would happen. Imran smiled as he settled down with Trash and was soon fast asleep.

Chapter Thirteen

A GOOD IDEA BACKFIRES

Trash made an excellent recovery and Eddie and Imran had a great deal of fun with her over the next few weeks. She seemed to have cured herself of the marble habit and now preferred mountains of cat food. Since her operation she seemed to have twice the energy she'd had before it. She was always taking herself off on adventures for hours at a time.

Charlie's lump was found to be just fatty tissue, a lymphoma, and had been easily and successfully removed from the tortoise's neck. Charlie was now back with her owner, living her adventurous and independent life.

One afternoon not long after the flood, Eddie went to the hospital as usual after school. It had now been fully cleaned although the roof had only been temporarily repaired because the insurance money had not been enough to complete all the necessary work. As Eddie entered he could hear the two vets arguing all the way down the corridor.

"Old Cheesy's in a stinking mood," he said to Chelsea.

"Yes, and guess who caused it?" she said, glaring pointedly at him. "Hilary's been trying to defend you, but you should have told someone first, Eddie."

Oh, dear. What had he done now?

"He wants to see you. Best get it over with," she said.

"But what have I done?" asked Eddie.

"Something to do with local newspapers?"

Blast! He'd almost forgotten about that. His secret phone calls before the flood had been to the local newspapers. Eddie had told them what he thought were interesting bits of information about the hospital. He had thought if he could get some publicity, people might start sending in donations and the hospital wouldn't be in such financial difficulty. But what had gone wrong?

*

Mr Wensleydale held up a newspaper in front of Eddie's nose. Despite Mr Wensleydale's hand shaking with rage, Eddie could still make out the headline:

"I telephoned the newspaper and they said that someone called Eddie Wright gave them the information," hissed Mr Wensleydale.

"Is it true, Eddie?" asked Hilary.

"Yes, it is true that Mr Wensleydale called the MP a turnip-head."

"You know what I mean," said Hilary. "Did you speak to the newspapers and tell them things about the hospital without asking us first?"

"I was only trying to help," said Eddie,

and explained his idea about getting publicity and donations. Unfortunately, the reporter hadn't mentioned anything about donations.

"This makes me look like a rude, loud-mouthed fool!" said Mr Wensleydale, his voice rising furiously.

You said it! Eddie wisely kept this thought to himself.

"Even if you were trying to help, the least you can do is apologise," said Hilary.

"I'm sorry," said Eddie.

"And you will go straight to the newspaper, now, and tell them that you made the whole thing up," said Mr Wensleydale, trying hard to contain his anger.

"Even though it's true?" asked Eddie.

"Especially because it is true," said Mr Wensleydale.

Half an hour later, Eddie had trudged up the steps of *The Clarion* office and was now talking to the local newspaper reporter, Andy Summers. Eddie had called home to ask Kate to go with him for a bit of moral support. She stood beside him, staring at Andy in a way that made the young reporter feel distinctly uncomfortable.

"So you want me to retract the whole thing, say it was all a lie?" asked Andy.

"Yes," said Eddie.

"Going to make me a look a bit of a twerp, isn't it?" said Andy.

Eddie thought that Andy looked more than a bit of a twerp. He thought he looked a complete twerp.

"We don't mind what you look like," said Kate.

"Will you do it?" Eddie asked.

"My editor wouldn't like it. Wouldn't like it at all."

"But there's been enough trouble there, what with the flood and everything. And if you don't, I might get banned from the hospital again," Eddie trailed off miserably.

Andy's little eyes sharpened.

"Flood! What flood? How come I didn't get to hear about it?" he said.

"Oh, yeah. It was dead dramatic! Me and Kate and loads of other kids helped to save the animals. And it was dangerous because Trash Cat, she belongs to my friend Imran, was having an operation while it was happening. Ace cat, she is."

Andy had his notebook out and was scribbling as fast as Eddie could talk. He was hooked. Kate gave a little smile.

"And the ceiling fell in and some kids

were crying with the cold. I had to keep diving down into metres of dirty water to make sure no one was trapped."

"And Mr Wensleydale . . . " Kate carried on, as Andy scribbled furiously.

"Cool it," hissed Eddie.

Kate stopped, and winked at Eddie.

Chapter Fourteen

TRASH THE HERO

Two days later Mr Wensleydale was a very confused man. He had decided to walk to work because it was a nice morning, because his wife had taken the car anyway, and because he needed the exercise. Not a man known for having a surplus of friends, he had been surprised because all the way to work people kept stopping to shake his hand. He vaguely thought that some of them were probably people who owned animals he had treated, but even that would not account for so much extraordinary behaviour.

"Well done, Mr Wensleydale."

"Keep up the good work."

"Brilliant. Absolutely first class."

"Congratulations."

"All the best."

Mr Wensleydale, who usually revelled in public attention, started to feel like a hunted animal and arrived at work in a thoroughly bad mood.

"Great news, eh, Mr Wensleydale?" said Chelsea cheerily as he passed through Reception.

Not her too. Was it some conspiracy? Some awful joke and everyone was having a good laugh at his expense? He slammed the door of his office, made a mug of coffee and settled down with his morning copy of *The Clarion*, a ritual he always enjoyed before starting the day's work, except when there was an emergency, of course. And that's when he saw the headline:

There was a large photograph of Trash Cat showing off her scar.

He read on:

During recent heavy rains, the ceiling of the Rainbow Animal Hospital collapsed and the whole place was flooded. The disaster was compounded by a complete power failure, leaving the terrified animals and staff cold, wet, and without heat or light. Human and animal lives were in constant danger. However, the staff behaved heroically. Together with local children they saved all the animals. One of the children, Eddie Wright, a saint-like volunteer worker at the hospital, and his angelic sister Kate, were both, said Mr Wensleydale, one of the vets, as "cool as cats" during the crisis. As was brave Trash, a cat who was undergoing major surgery when the skies fell in and the power failed. She has now fully recovered. It is a shame that in our so-called caring community, a want of funds for repair work meant that the roof leaked so badly the hospital was flooded and many lives were put at at risk.

Mr Wensleydale put down the paper. He absently swigged a great mouthful of hot coffee and burnt his mouth. Eddie Wright. Eddie Wright. The boy's name rang like some awful curse in his mind. What could he do about that boy?

There was a knock at the door.

"Come," said Mr Wensleydale.

The door opened and there was Eddie, Kate, a smiling Andy Summers and a photographer. Kalim and Hilary were with them.

"Congratulations," said Andy Summers.

"On what exactly?" asked Mr Wensleydale.

Andy smiled again.

"After my little piece on the cat in the flood this morning, my editor decided to show the way by donating two hundred and fifty pounds to your hospital. Readers took the hint. Up to now we've had forty phone calls. I reckon you're going to make a couple of thousand from this. Good publicity for the paper. You get your roof done and a bit on the side. Not bad, eh?"

Mr Wensleydale was led outside to pose with Eddie and Kate for a photograph. What else could he do?

Chapter Fifteen

A Scare and a Happy Event

A few weeks later Eddie received a telephone call from Imran who was nearly in tears. Eddie raced around to his friend's house on his bike and Imran led him upstairs. Under his bed Trash was lying on her side.

"What's up?" asked Eddie.

"She's done it again, only worse this time," said Imran.

Not more marbles!

Eddie felt her stomach gently, and sure enough she did seem to have swallowed something pretty big. Giant marbles, perhaps.

"They'll have to operate again, won't they?" asked Imran.

"Don't worry," said Eddie. "Let's just get her to the hospital as quick as we can."

They put Trash in the pet carrier and cycled to the hospital.

"Not again," said Chelsea. "Isn't she ever going to learn?"

They took Trash straight through to Hilary as an emergency. Trash was barely moving and had a strange look on her face. Eddie hoped that she wasn't going to lose consciousness. Hilary took Trash out of the carrier and examined her.

"It's worse than last time, isn't it?" asked Imran, miserably.

"No, it's much, much better," said Hilary.

The two boys looked at each other.

"But is it marbles, or what?" asked Eddie.

"Not marbles, Eddie," said Hilary. "Kittens!"

And so the kittens came. A tabby one, two blackish grey ones, two ginger and white ones, and the last was a little fellow with splodges of grey, black, ginger and white who seemed very surprised at being in the world.

"Splodge," said Imran. "I'll call him Splodge."

Trash licked them until they were all dry

and fluffy. Then she licked Eddie and Imran and Hilary, until she was so tired she went to sleep. She needed to, because her new family was going to keep her very busy from now on.

Enjoy more great stories from

Rainbow ANIMAL HOSPITAL

Toffee's Big Problem

Coming soon!

Eddie screamed. He couldn't help himself. He had never known pain like it.

"Aaagh! Get her off!"

It all happened so quickly. No one had expected it. Not the owner of the cat, not Greg the trainee nurse, and not Eddie, who, as usual, was spending as much out-of-school time as he could at the Rainbow Animal Hospital.

*

In all his eleven years, Eddie had never seen anything like it. He was frightened, but he kept his nerve, even when the claws dug in so deeply he thought he might pass out. The cat was a tabby called Jemimah and was normally quite docile. Her owner, Peggy, a shy woman with a kind smile, had brought her in that morning. The poor cat suffered from fits, or seizures, and they were becoming more frequent. Drugs had been of little help, so Jemimah had come into the hospital for a brain scan. The chief vet Mr Wensleydale, or old Cheesy as Eddie called him, thought she might be epileptic. In the Treatment Room Greg had just taken Jemimah out of her pet carrier. As he put her on the table and turned to speak to Peggy, the cat suddenly hissed and seemed to somersault over and on to her side. Eddie made a grab to stop her falling off the table and she sunk her front claws into his right hand.

Peggy and Greg managed to get Jemimah off Eddie, but only after he had received three deep, nasty gashes. Jemimah was now on her back, clawing the air, foam and spittle coming from her mouth. Her whole body was twitching as if electric shocks were being sent through her. Even though Eddie was shocked at what had happened, and his hand was throbbing painfully, he still wanted the cat's suffering to stop. Clutching his bleeding hand he ran off to find Mr Wensleydale.

"What is it? I'm busy," the vet said irritably as he sat at his desk trying to make sense of a mountain of bills.

"It's Jemimah the cat. She's had a fit. You've got to come quick. I..." Eddie paused as a wave of nausea washed over him. Mr Wensleydale looked up, took in Eddie's white, strained face, his bleeding hand, and got up without saying a word. He walked swiftly along, followed by Eddie, and gave Jemimah an injection to subdue her. Her eyes were rolling horribly and she seemed to be in a world of pain far removed from the Rainbow Animal Hospital. As the injection quickly took hold, Jemimah quietened. Peggy was in tears, because of the fit and because of what had happened to Eddie.

"I'm so sorry, I'm so sorry," she repeated over and over again.

"It wasn't her fault. She couldn't help it," Eddie said, and realised the pain in his hand had now brought tears to his own eyes. He blinked them back furiously.

Greg bathed Eddie's hand in warm

water and antiseptic, then Mr Wensleydale looked at the deep wounds.

"Hospital for you. You'll need a few stitches," he said. "It had to be you at the centre of the drama, didn't it?" Mr Wensleydale added irritably.

Then he turned to Greg.

"And I'll see you in my office after work. You should know better than to put an unqualified person at risk."

Greg knew better than to argue. Eddie was about to say something when Greg gave him a shut-up-things-are-bad-enough-as-it-is look. Eddie felt awful. Greg had been in a pretty quiet mood lately and now he was in trouble with Mr Wensleydale because of Eddie. Mr Wensleydale never really approved of Eddie being in the Hospital and this wasn't going to help. Chelsea, Eddie's elder sister who worked in Reception, was given time off to take Eddie to hospital.

"I don't know why one of the vets couldn't have stitched me up," Eddie said in the minicab. "I mean, they're allowed to do people, aren't they?"

"You never know, they might catch something from you!" Chelsea said.

From

Toffee's Big Problem

Look out for it!

Order Form

To order books direct from the publishers, just make a list of the titles you want and send it with your name and address to:

Dept 6,
HarperCollins Publishers Ltd,
Westerhill Road,
Bishopbriggs,
Glasgow G64 2QT

Please enclose a cheque or postal order to the value of the cover price, plus:

UK and BFPO: Add £1 for the first book, and 25p per copy for each additional book ordered.

Overseas and Eire: Add £2.95 service charge. Books will be sent by surface mail, but quotes for airmail despatch will be given on request.

A 24-hour telephone ordering service is available to Visa and Access card holders on 0141-772 2281.